JamDown Sto

S Calliard

Cover Design: Joseph Shepherd

Illustrator: Joseph Shepherd

Copyright © 2019 by Sonia Calliard

All rights reserved. No part of this book may be reproduced, stored in a retrieval system, or transmitted in any form or by any means, including electronic, mechanical, photocopying, recording or otherwise without the prior written permission of the author.

Introduction

This book is a collection of short stories featuring a fictional community who live in Guava Ground, Clarendon, Jamaica WI. Guava Ground is actually a real place, and is where my family are from on my mother's side. I have heard many stories from relatives about growing up there and this has provided inspiration for my book. Furthermore, I love West Indian food and came up with the idea to base my characters on my favourite foods.

Briefly, Guava Ground is a village in Crofts Hill, which is in the parish of Clarendon, Jamaica, WI. Clarendon is located in the county of Middlesex. Jamaica is divided into 3 counties; Middlesex, Cornwall and Surrey, and each county is further divided into parishes. Each parish has a capital town. Two parish capitals, Montego Bay in St. James and Kingston, have city status. Kingston is also the capital of Jamaica.

Middlesex county has 5 parishes: Saint Ann (capital - St Anne's Bay), St Catherine (capital - Spanish Town), Clarendon (capital - May Pen), Manchester (capital - Mandeville), Saint Mary (capital - Port Maria).

Cornwall county is also made up of 5 parishes: Saint Elizabeth (capital - Black River), Trelawney (capital - Falmouth), Hanover (capital - Lucea), Westmoreland (capital - Savanna-la-Mar), Saint James (capital - Montego Bay).

Surrey county has 4 parishes: Portland (capital - Port Antonio), Saint Andrew (capital - Half-Way Tree), Saint Thomas (capital - Morant Bay), Kingston (capital - Kingston).

Okay, Geography lesson over, let's get back to the book.

Warning to Readers! This book is about fictional characters and in no way are they meant to represent any real people, near or far! It is not always politically correct. If you anticipate that you are going to be offended, then you have the freedom of choice to stop reading now. If you continue reading and then feel offended, I will not accept responsibility, as you have had prior warning. Furthermore, get used to reading patios. I won't explain every phrase so it is your responsibility to learn Jamaican/Caribbean phrases.

Now, before I begin, I would like to introduce some of the characters I will be featuring in my stories...

Chris Cassava (bammy) aka Flats (short for flatbread) – grounded and good natured.
Miss Bammy – a well-respected local resident (Chris Cassava's mother).
Johnnie Cake (fried dumpling) – local Music Producer.
Fiona Festival (long shaped, sweet fried dumpling) – pleasant and down to earth
Turna Cornmeal (turn cornmeal) – facety, two-faced gal.
Latoya Likkle Foot (chicken foot) – Turna Cornmeal's skinny, dry-skin friend.
Maas Run Down (Run Down) – him love a gal!
Souse (Bajan dish made with pork) – Maas Run Down's Bajan friend.

Bulla Brown (bulla cake) – fat and lazy, used to be the school bully but too lazy to even try that now.

Tilla Toto (toto) aka Killa Toto – she likkle but she tallawah!

Benny & Jenny Fritter (fritters) – from the Fritter family, stalwarts of the community.

Mr Moss (Irish moss) – Irish immigrant, married to a Jamaican.

Miss Sweetie (sweet potato pudding) – birth name Portia Pudding.

Gogo Gizada (gizada) – local resident and entrepreneur; owns a Go-Go bar and massage parlour.

Mrs Priscilla Pear (prickly pear) – nickname Prickly Pear, due to her very haughty attitude.

Quinty Dumpling (fried knot dumpling) – she ton up!

Jerks (jerk chicken) – de girls seh him love-making hot like fire!

Cliff Cowcod (cow cod soup) – undercover male escort.

Pattie L'Bell (Jamaican patty) – famous reggae star from the local district.

Pastor Lickie Lickie (real name Dick Likkle) – gravalishus Pastor.

Banana Dread (banana bread) – the local Dread.

Spanish Fly (aphrodisiac) – a real Spanish fly, blown off course during winter migration a year ago, ending up in Jamaica. Lives in Banana Dread's mango tree and recently branched out to set up office in the Dread's banana tree.

JamDown Stories is essentially a work in progress, and not all the characters listed above are featured in this first book. I will be releasing new stories as I develop the characters, so enjoy the book and watch out for more antics from the JamDown Crew!

BRUK OUT!

This is a very short story introducing Pastor Lickie Lickie and some of his parishena...

Pastor Lickie Lickie has been on vacation to the USA a few times and now has the annoying tendency of lapsing into an American accent as if he was born there.

Pastor Lickie Lickie's birth name is Dick Likkle. His father, Mr Lambert Likkle, liked the actor Dirk Bogart and decided to name his baby son Dirk Bogart Likkle, but you know how things go in the West Indies. His parents weren't too good with spelling and pronunciation...and the Registrar mistook the r for a c, and registered him as Dick Likkle! Mr Likkle Senior didn't realise until a few months after the birth was registered, when a family member, who could spell and pronounce words well, pointed out in front of others that the child's name was in fact Dick, not Dirk. Mr Likkle Senior went down the registry office the next day and cuss two bad wod pon de Registrar! Not that it did any good. He called his son Dirk despite the registrar's mistake, and insisted everyone else did too. They did, but only when he was present. After a while they stopped bothering and called him Dick regardless. Well, it was really because Dick's grandmother Miss Mavis – his father's mother – said she couldn't care less wheh him waan seh, Dick easier fi pronongs so a dat she ah call him. She added that if him farder no happy wid it him can gweh, caah she barn him and him caahn tell she weh fi seh. She concluded by stating she noh know why de man did waahn fi call him son such a heediat name an' ef him did pick a sensible

name like weh she did tell him, him would'n have people a laugh after him! She lamented that she had wanted her grandson named after her late husband, Halston Silbert Likkle, which would have been a much more sensible option.
She concluded, "Well. When wata t'row weh, it cyan pick up back." (What's done is done.)

I digress. As I was saying, this is a short, short, introduction...

Pastor Lickie Lickie is a widower; his beloved wife died 5 years ago. So far, he has been unsuccessful in finding another wife from his congregation. He has had a few offers but he hasn't found a woman who he feels matches up to his late wife, Mrs Deirdre Likkle. To begin with, she was the best cook he has ever met. She made him so happy. She would cook all his favourite dishes; and she kept a lovely home. She didn't have to work; the congregation tithes provided for them well, and he drove a top of the range car. Oh yes, his congregation was a faithful flock! He reminded himself often that he was very fortunate.

The pastor thought wistfully that he was no longer a young man. In his young days he was wild (according to him). He drank, smoked and had lots of girlfriends. All that changed when he was caught in bed with his boss's wife, when he was supposed to be at work and the boss came home early. Boss man run fi him gun, and pastor Lickie Lickie run fi him trousers!! The speed at which he fled that house was the subject of gossip for years afterwards. Some say they never even see him pass them, they just felt a gust of wind and saw lots of dust swirling about as some great force whooshed by.

It's surprising how many people turn to the church after one too many close calls. Pastor Lickie Lickie was one of them. After his escape he vowed to change, and change he did…well not exactly same time, but within the next few years. Okay, so he got older, fatter and lazier and the women lost interest, basically, so he joined the church to looked for a wife to settle down with. After joining the church, he found he enjoyed the thrill of seeing women swooning over his voice when he spoke from the pulpit. He discovered he had a lovely baritone voice which was very soothing and commanding, and he was asked regularly to read from the scriptures and lead the singing. He decided to use his gift and he joined the ministry to train as a preacher. And no, he still insists his decision was not in any way influenced by the big house and fancy car that belonged to the minister of the church at that time; the one he used to stare at in wonder and envy.

Despite his loneliness, Pastor Lickie Lickie has been scared off by certain women joining the church in order to find themselves a "good Christian man". He has lost count of the number of propositions made to him by these women, which are becoming more suggestive! They know he lives alone in a fine, big, comfortable house and is financially secure.

One time fight even bruk out at the Likkle Saviour Divine Evangelist Pentecostal Church Charity Auction between Miss Battie and Miss Bench when they went head to head in a bidding war for a date with the Pastor. Dem cuss some bad word in de place, you see!! It did bad! Miss Battie pull off Miss Bench burgundy wig, and Miss Bench take her handbag and give Miss Battie one raaaas lick when she couldn't grab de wig back from de damn woman! Me seh people put down some belly laugh dat day when de two woman start fi rumble. De woman dem en' up pon di floor and people start tek bet as to which one goin win de fight.

Some of the church Elders were outraged at the bad behaviour. Dem get out dem bible and start fi quote scripture. Some people try bruk up de fight and get box by Miss Bench handbag. She tek it and she start swing it like cricket bat, cah you know by dis time she BEX!!! She noh even business bout she fake Brazilian wig weh she pay so much money fah. Me seh!! When she mek one swing an lick Miss Battie, somebody bawl out "6!" Ahh bwoy, dat was a day to remember.

Then there is Miss Plantain. She's always hinting that she needs a nice man to look after, and telling Pastor Lickie Lickie he needs a woman like her to massage him after a hard day preaching and doing the Lord's work. She even offered him a trial run, promising she could reach parts others can't! Pastor Lickie Lickie, in his weaker moments, has often thought about taking her up on the offer, but he has not yet succumbed.

Instead, he has been praying hard for a sign that things will improve in his search for a wife and asking for deliverance from the current pool of would-be suiters.

"Gawd," he prayed, "please guide and protec' me."

"There was a time when I woulda glad fi ooman fight over me. But I mended me ways many years ago, praise de Lawd. Now me jus waan peace and quiet and someone fi cook and clean fi me, an' be a company when I need it." (Does that sound like a wife, or a glorified housekeeper? You decide! Sorry, I'm interjecting).

"Lawd hear di plea of your humble servant. Please send me a nice woman, but not none ah dem in me church!!"

"Lawd, she don' haffi too pretty, but please me noh waan no ole bruk. Fagive me, I apologise fi me language. You know bes' oh Lawd. Please send me a sign when she goin' come. I am lonely and in need of comfort since me wonderful Deirdre pass. Please hear me prayer and don' leave me too long in me misry."

"Amen."

Hmmm... I goin' fin' someone fi fix him business! Watch! Soon come.

BANANA DREAD AND THE RASTA PIE

Banana Dread woke up one bright morning and decided he was going to make his favourite dish, Rasta Pie. He lived on a small plot of land which had a mango tree that bore the sweetest mangos in the neighbourhood, according to locals. Banana Dread also had a noni tree which bore noni fruit (yuk! awful tasting fruit) that he used as a natural remedy for curing all manner of ailments. Banana Dread had a banana tree too, and an orange tree. He grew a host of foods such as okra, breadfruit, pumpkin and callaloo.

He loved nothing more than picking ripe fruit from his trees and eating them while he lounged in his hammock daydreaming about faraway lands. Banana Dread is always talking about Ethiopia, the Fatherland. Prickly Pear always says she doesn't know why he doesn't just pick up himself and go to Africa if he loves it that much! One day, when she heard him talking about Africa yet again, she exclaimed!
"Why you noh gwaan ah Hafrica! An mek lion and tiger niam you! Cho, me no inna dis Rastafari business."
She complained, "Me no understan' why unnu dreadlocks man always ah talk 'bout Africa, Farderland, dis an dat, an no matter 'ow much time unnu gittup an siddung, unno no put one foot outa Jamaica yet! Mek you noh gallang?!"

I'm going off on a tangent again; back to the story...

Banana Dread put on his favourite tune, "Day Dreaming of Africa" by Lloyd Jones, and started

getting things out of his cupboards to make the pie. Every time he made Rasta Pie it had different ingredients, according to what he could find, dig up or acquire at any given time. He should have called it 'Fling Anyting In' pie, or 'Anyting Me Find' pie. Mostly his pie consisted of vegetables only, and sometimes they included fish. He went outside in the yard to collect some of the ingredients for the pie. He spotted Spanish Fly stretched out chillaxing in his mango tree, as if to say "See me yah!"
"Damn fly!" He said to himself.
"From 'im come 'im jus ah stalk people fi dem food. Me ah go set fi him, you watch." He cursed to himself. Then he called out, "You still deh yah?! Weh mek you no dead? De amount a lick you get, you still ah hover roun de place!"
Spanish fly stretched and yawned, and thought, "A weh mek dat bwoy always a cuss me. Hafta me noh trouble 'im more dan so."
He fired back at the Dread, "Gweh, an' stap you noise, Banana Bwoy!"

Banana Dread kissed his teeth and continued to gather up the ingredients for his pie. He muttered to himself, "Me gwine deal wid dat dutty fly before de day finish."
He finished collecting the ingredients for the pie and set to work on it. He baked the pie in his little oven and when it was well-cooked, he took it out and put it on the table top to cool while he got out his plate and knife and fork. Banana Dread was so engrossed he forgot all about Spanish Fly, and did not notice when the fly flew in and perched himself on the table beside the pie. Something told Banana Dread to look up, and he saw Spanish Fly squatting by his pie. Banana Dread was vexed. He made one lick after Spanish Fly

with the kitchen towel he had in his hand...BLAP! It caught Spanish Fly on his head an' mash up him new cap weh 'im jus' get from America; the special edition SoniaC gold label classic design (you know Jamaicans love name-brand!). Spanish Fly see red!! Him pay nuff dollars fi de cap an' it mash up.
Him warn, "Banana Bwoy, you dead now!"
Him draw fi him cutlass and shout, "Bwoy, you tink me easy! Me gwine gi you some dreadnaught blows!" Spanish Fly swooped at Banana Dread, cutlass raised, and swiped at him (which obviously didn't do much because we all know a fly is much smaller than a Banana!). You should have seen the two of them in the place, Spanish Fly swooping and Banana Dread jumping and dancing about flicking his tea towel wildly, trying to knock out the fly; who managed somehow to bite Banana Dread on his bottom, secreting enough poison to cause an itchy swelling. Banana Dread felt the prick and stopped momentarily to rub his behind. Spanish Fly took the opportunity to fly off and headed straight for Banana Dread's Rasta Pie (Nooo!). Spanish Fly looked back at Banana Dread with a smirk.
"Now, see weh you ah go do," he goaded.
"You ah go pay fi me cap. You tek dis ting fi joke!"

Banana Dread, whose rear end had started to swell and itch, was furious to see the fly hovering and about to land on his beloved pie. He grabbed an old newspaper, rolled it up, took aim and brought it down hard. Spanish Fly deftly dodged the paper weapon of destruction and it came down hard on the pie...BAM!! The pastry was shattered, and the contents of the pie splattered everywhere. Banana Dread's Rasta Pie was ruined, and so was his appetite. He threw the remains of the pie out into the yard.

Spanish Fly gorged himself on Rasta Pie that day til 'im belly bung, and dined on it for an entire week afterwards! He is still cursing Banana Dread for mashing up his designer cap though. As for Banana Dread, he was so vex and upset that he went to bed hungry, had a sore arse for a week and is setting for Spanish Fly next time.

Too Lickie Lickie

Pastor Lickie Lickie sat back in his chair, after having accepted another dinner invitation from one of his parishioners. He thanked his prospective hosts, a local carpenter and his wife, for their kind invitation and agreed that he would see them next Sunday after church service at 4pm. It was Tuesday night, and he was preparing to go on another conversion mission. A conversion mission involved visiting various dens of iniquity in the community to try to turn the shady individuals inside away from their blaspheming life of sin and debauchery toward a new, God-fearing existence. Basically, he wanted to persuade more people to join his church. More members meant more tithes! Tonight, he had decided to go to the new go-go bar which had opened up on the edge of town. He had heard some of his congregation discussing this new venue between themselves and commenting about what went on in there. This repulsed (and excited) him. For shame, he had to say a silent prayer every time he thought of it.

That night he gathered a group of his most trusted elders (people who could keep a secret), and they made their way to the club. Pastor Lickie Lickie walked into the go-go bar on a mission to preach to the girls working there. When he walked in his eyes nearly popped out of his head. He was transfixed. One of the elders had to nudge him to remind him what he was there to do. Pastor Lickie Lickie began preaching, "Lord have mercy on these poor lost souls," he cried out.
"Let them repent and turn away from evil."
Someone piped up, "Wait, me noh see you in 'ere last week Pastor?!"

All the girls laughed.
"Not me, never. I will not forsake my faith to such debauchery!" The pastor exclaimed. Then a movement in the corner caught his eye and he looked closer. "Brother Moss!" He called out.
"What you doin' in here? An' me jus' see you inna church last week wid you lovely wife!"
"Come out an' go home!"
Mr Moss emerged sheepishly from behind a large sofa and scurried away.

Pastor Lickie Lickie turned his attention once more to the people in the club. He was about to begin speaking again when he felt a tap on his shoulder. He turned around and saw standing before him the most radiant, sexy, mature woman he had ever set his big greedy eyes upon. It was Gogo Gizada, or Queen G, as she is commonly known in the parish. Ms Gizada addressed Pastor Lickie Lickie in a husky, velvet voice.
"Good evening, Pastor."
Pastor Lickie Lickie stood before her, transfixed, while she mesmerised him with her eyes. He felt as if she was drinking in every part of him. Then she spoke again. "Pastor, I was hoping I would bump into you."
"I understand the hard work you are doing to turn all the poor sinners away from evil and bring them into the light."
While she spoke, her ample chest moved up and down. Pastor Lickie Lickie contained himself and began fervently praying to save his soul from eternal damnation.
"I can see dat you work very hard helping others," Miss Gizada purred.
"I tink you need to de-stress."

"I want to invite you to sample the clean, refreshing delights of a relaxing, de-toxifying massage at my newly-opened massage parlour on Boulevard Street."

While she spoke, he kept his eyes above her neck. Pastor Lickie Lickie knew he needed to reach out to his flock, not to Queen G's ample assets! His mind wandered. He could vaguely make out that she was explaining that her current establishment was not the demonic den of ill-repute he assumed it to be. It was a place where adults of both sexes came to relax and unwind, to have a drink and to sample good home cooked food; where they could watch fabulous live entertainment. She also had an exclusive venue where clients of both sexes could enjoy a detoxifying massage by trained staff. Somehow, Pastor Lickie Lickie found himself agreeing to accept her kind invitation to sample her Premium Massage Service on Boulevard Street, administered by her very self! In return, she pledged to give a donation to his church to help with their charity work with disadvantaged children in the community. How could he turn her down?

The church Elders who accompanied him were less than convinced. However, he reassured them by reminding them that their Saviour had lived among the people and worked with sinners to save them from eternal damnation and that is exactly what he is doing.

The next day Pastor Lickie Lickie attended Queen G's Majestic Splendor Unisex Massage Parlour as arranged. When he arrived, Queen G welcomed him warmly. She guided him into a sumptuously decorated private sitting room, complete with elegant comfy armchair and mood lighting. She instructed him to disrobe (tek off him clothes), and handed him a beautifully soft, luxurious velvet bathrobe to put on. She hung his clothes in the custom-made wooden locker provided. The sitting room led directly to a private massage/therapy room which was just the right temperature. It was beautifully decorated with expensive designer wallpaper and a plush chaise longue (don't be ignorant and ask what a 'chez longe' is, look it up!). Soft relaxing music was playing in the background. Essential burning oils spread their intoxicating perfume which swirled around the room. Queen G assured the Pastor that only esteemed, respectable clientele visited her salon. She kept her prices high in order to deter "certain hellements" who may come and lower the standard of her business. "An' we noh waahnt dat, do we Pastor..." she purred. "Oh goodness, no", blustered the Pastor.

Queen G informed him that she had lined up one of her more mature and experienced ladies to attend to him, but she had remembered she had promised to deal with him herself, so she was going to change into her uniform and would be with him shortly. She returned wearing a crisp white one-piece button front uniform dress which fitted perfectly to every contour of her coca cola body (check out the tune from Simpleton – Coca-Cola Bottle Shape. Da soun' deh Mad!!). The Pastor was hypnotised. Queen G snapped him out of his stupor.
"Right Pastor, time for your treatment." She said briskly.
She began putting him through his paces by showing him the male massage bed (...wait, me ah come to it!!). When she explained what the centre hole in the bed was for, he hardly flinched; that's because he wasn't really listening! She explained that they called it the

'man-hole'. She showed him how to position himself the correct way on the bed, and assured him nothing untoward would happen. It was purely for his comfort and was designed by a top furniture designer specifically for their male customers, and at great cost. She told him female customers obviously did not need such a bed but, based on customer feedback, massage beds had been specially designed for their female customers too. Queen G left Pastor Lickie Lickie for five minutes to give him time to undress, cover himself with a large towel and position himself on the bed, before knocking to see if it was okay for her to come back in. He bid her enter, and boy did she get down to work. In no time at all the Pastor was in a pleasure-induced stupor. Queen G rubbed his shoulders, back and legs with a speciality oil she called Sweet Dream. Soon he was very sleepy and felt himself drifting off. He thought he saw through half-closed eyes Queen G bend down and go under the massage bed, but he could have been mistaken. Then he felt a disturbing and wonderful rippling sensation which started from the pit of his stomach and spread downwards. He didn't know if he was dreaming or not but, holy mercy, he didn't want it to end. He wondered if being in heaven would be just as marvellous. If it was, he would be happy never to wake up. All of a sudden, he experienced such a wonderfully explosive sensation that spread throughout the whole of his body, from the top of his balding head to the tips of his size 11 feet. He thought he had died and gone to his last wonderful resting place where he would reside forever, Amen! Then he remembered nothing more.

What seemed like an eternity later, he felt himself being shaken gently awake. Grudgingly, he opened his eyes. He did not want to come back to reality. Queen G's kind face loomed before him.

"Wake up, Pastor, your massage is over." She told him.

"You been asleep for an hour, and I have another client appointment."

Pastor Lickie Lickie understood why clients would come back again and again. He didn't fully understand what happened to him, but he knew he would never forget the experience. He couldn't help feeling that perhaps something sinful might have occurred, but he couldn't quite put his finger on it. He pushed the uneasy feeling aside as he got up and dressed himself. Queen G was waiting outside the room for him. He thanked her for her attentiveness and excellent service, and reminded her of her pledge to donate to his church. She did so right away, handing him a fat envelope, and asked him to come again, stating, "Your pleasure is our pleasure!"

Pastor Lickie Lickie bid Queen G farewell, tipped his trilby hat and said he might just do that. Queen G watched him walk away and chuckled to herself. She had no doubt he would be back. She had a 100% success rate!

KILLA IN THE VILLA

Killa Toto (real name Tilla Toto) was practising her lyrics for her next appearance at the local reggae talent show. She was the up and coming talent in the district. She had been discovered by Johnny Cake, who was trying to persuade her to make him her manager. She knew he had dollar signs in his eyes every time he closed them. Although she had to admit to herself that he was a shrewd businessman and did make money for his clients, she was in no rush to get on his books! She had other plans.

She began to write...

Me short, me sweet,
Me know how fi do-it,
Hear me now people
Mek we rock to de beat.
Me deh pon top,
An me nah go stop
Me ah ride dis yah wave
So mek de riddim drop...

Listen me noh!...

Me no inna dutti wine,
Me ongle sweet wine,
Cah me rock in time
Mek you eye dem shine,
While we rock in time,
To di sweet reggae vibe.

Move from side to side,
Unnu watch de ride,

Mek we dip an slide,
Like we have some pride,

Me seh you 'ave some gal,
Weh no understan'
Dem ah do dutti wine
Pon all type a man,

Dem flash all weh dem 'ave,
An ah gwaan bad,
But me haffi aks,
Weh do you gal, you mad!

When you check it out,
Dem have too much mout',
Instead a earn respec',
Dem jus' a fling all bout.

Just then there was a knock at the door, which made her jump as she was concentrating so much. It was Johnny Cake.
"Cho!" Tilla said to herself.
She forgot he was coming over to her home to ask her grandmother, Miss Sour Sop, if he could be her manager. Killa rolled her eyes. She didn't need a manager. She was happy just taking part in local competitions for fun without any added pressures. Besides, she had her High School studies to think about. She wanted to be a scientist. She loved science; chemistry, biology, physics. Taking part in these small local competitions was just a hobby to her. She was not going to abandon her education to help line Johnny Cake's pockets!
"No," she decided, "Me nah mek 'im manage me 'career'."
"Him nah manage notn, period!"

Just then, she heard her grandmother call out, "A who a knock me door so loud eeehhh?!!"
She heard Johnny Cake reply "Is me, Mr Johnny Cake, Miss Sour Sop. Me come fi talk some business wid you."

Miss Sour Sop was Killa Toto's maternal grandmother. She was a shrewd and clever woman with a sharp tongue and business mind who had done well for herself, considering she had no schooling beyond the age of 13 when she had to go out to work to help support her family after her own mother died. She managed to acquire a couple of shops that were doing very well. She also built and rented out a couple of houses to professional tenants, as well as building her own spacious home with her late husband, which she shared with Tilla and Tilla's mother, Quinty Dumpling.

Due to Miss Sour Sop's own hard life, she was determined that her granddaughter would finish her schooling, and she was prepared to make whatever sacrifices she needed to, to make sure Tilla succeeded in any profession she decided to follow. Miss Sour Sop considered that her own daughter, Quinty, had wasted her good education, and was spending too much time running down man (in Miss Sour Sop's opinion!) – or in other words, dating - instead of settling down with a good husband. Quinty's argument was that if she met a man of the same calibre as her father, she might consider settling down! Quinty was a talented dressmaker, and was making a reasonable living from designing and making one-off couture garments, when she could be bothered. In fact, Quinty was good at most things she turned her hand to, but she just couldn't stick to any one thing. She also discovered she had a natural talent in the art of seduction, but let's not go there.

Miss Sour Sop called her a Jack of all trades, Master of none.

"Jack av all trade, Master av notn," were her words, to be precise.

Miss Sour Sop despaired of her only daughter. She had held hopes of Quinty becoming a Barrister or a Judge, or someone of equal high standing. She had all but given up on Quinty fulfilling her true potential, but she had faith in her granddaughter Tilla who was more down to earth and studious, unlike her mother. Tilla was much more focused and sensible as far as her grandmother was concerned.

One thing about Quinty though, she did not take any rubbish from any male suiter. She had her standards and she accepted nothing less than curtesy and respect. Her father had taught her, by example, how a man should behave. Quinty witnessed a close and loving relationship between her parents right up until the day Maas Sop passed away suddenly eight years previous. It was a dreadful shock for the family, and she was sure her mother had not got over it to this day. He was a calm, softly spoken man; a keen gardener and cultivator, and talented musician. Quinty took comfort in knowing his musical talent had passed to her dear daughter, Tilla. Quinty had not yet found her forever Mr Right, but for the moment she was enjoying herself searching for him! She was in no great rush to settle down. Truth be told, she had her heart broken when Tilla's father broke off their engagement just before she discovered she was pregnant and, although she has had a couple of serious relationships since then, she has never forgotten her first love. No-one has ever come close to her ideal as far as she is concerned. Miss Sour Sop keeps telling her she's going to pick an' pick til she pick sh*t.

Tilla had already mentioned to her mother and grandmother about Johnnie Cake's plan to visit. Quinty decided she would take full advantage of the situation. Johnnie Cake didn't know it yet, but he was going to be Quinty's next project. She did love a challenge! She knew her mother did not approve of the music industry, and that Miss Sour Sop would send him on his way empty handed faster than you could say "gimme de contract!" She was going to let her mother do her worst, then she would step in and 'rescue' the situation.

Now, Quinty saw more to Johnnie Cake than she cared to admit. He was attractive, charming and polite, and he had his own money, which is not a bad combination! Quinty set about making a plan. She told Miss Sour Sop she would handle the great Johnnie Cake, as after all it was her daughter he was coming to talk about. Miss Sour Sop was having none of it. She knew Quinty was up to something, but she didn't care because she was not going to let Johnny Cake influence her granddaughter to neglect her studies. She had high hopes for Tilla.

Miss Sour Sop gave Johnnie Cake precisely three minutes to attempt to convince her about managing Tilla, before she cut him off and told him in no uncertain terms that Tilla would pursue a singing career over her dead body and she didn't count on dying any time soon. She walked him to the porch and sent him on his way.

"Listen me, Missa Cake," she said, drawing herself up to her full height of 5 foot zero inches, "I am a professional business woman, an' my granddaughter goin grow up to be a professional sommady. An believe me, it nah go be as no bim-bam singer, girating 'erself around half naked fi mek people tek hadvantage."

"No Missa Cake, dat naah go happen. Me allow she fi enter singing competition fi have likkle fun, but me noh mean seh she fi really tek dat ting fi serious career and give up har studies. No sah!" She was adamant.

"So, tank you fi comin, sorry you wase up you time, but no tanks!"

Johnny Cake started to smooth talk Miss Sour Sop, trying to get her to change her mind. As she was a successful business woman, he reasoned, she could see the potential in her granddaughter to make a lot of money, maybe even become a big star and be in a position to help her family financially.

Miss Sour Sop stopped him, "Listen me, young man."

"Fi me descendant nah go sing an flaunt harself like some ah dem let loose leggo-beast gal out deh fi money, no care how much!!!"

She continued to mutter to herself, "Me hope she put as much effort inna she book as she do ah mek up sing-song."

Johnny Cake knew better than to argue with Miss Sour Sop at that particular time. He bid her a good afternoon and walked away determined to formulate another plan to get around her, and Killa Toto!

Tilla heard the front door bang shut and heard her grandmother's footsteps coming towards her room. "Tilla!" Miss Sour Sop called out.

"No badda get mix up inna dis entertainment business and neglec' you bookwork! You 'ere me?! Cah me no spen' money fi sen' you go a school ongle fi you bruk out pon me!!! You 'ere me Tilla!" She continued.
"Yes Granma. Me nah go do dat, Mam. Me a go finish me education. Me jus' like fi sing sometimes fi fun Granma, ah noh notn serious, Mam." Tilla replied.
"Good!" Exclaimed Miss Sour Sop.
"An I tell dat man noh fi badda come roun' again! 'Im mek enough money fram people. Me no want him "manage you career" so 'im seh. Mek 'im gwaan! Me waant you fi pass you exam and go a Harvard an dem ting deh, and go get doctored."
"You mean get my doctorate, Mam." Tilla corrected.
"You know weh me mean! Hafter dis competition you ah go stop sing; you haffi sit hexam soon, so you haffi stop de extra-carricilar activity, me ah warn you!"
"Yes, Mam," Tilla answered.
Tilla knew her grandmother was right, and only had her best interests at heart. She would have to stop singing after this competition and concentrate on her studies, as she had important exams coming up and she wanted to do well and get into a good University.

Meanwhile, as Johnny Cake was walking away from the house, he heard someone call his name softly. He turned around to see Quinty Dumpling walking towards him slowly, swaying her hips as she sidled up to him.
"Hi Mr Johnnie Cake," she greeted him.
"Me 'ere you an' me mudda."
Johnny couldn't help but notice her long legs in her shorts and her close-fitting top. He was afraid of Quinty, because she always looked lovely and she aroused his carnal desires. He never liked to mix business with pleasure. He knew it would take much effort to resist her and that he would have to keep his

guard up. He was determined not to fall for her charms.

"You shoulda come when Mama Sop was out." Quinty laughed her soft laugh and Johnny Cake felt himself melting. He didn't know what to say.

"I tell you what," she said.

"Come pick me up later, mek we go somewhere private to discuss you plans for Tilla. After all, me ah she mudda an ah me you shoulda talk to."

Johnny Cake studied Quinty while his brain began to calculate. He was reluctant to be alone with her, but he was a greedy money-grabbing…I mean, a shrewd businessman, and could see the potential in Tilla to make them both a bag of money. He eventually agreed to meet with Quinty the next day. Tilla knew nothing of her mother's scheming. As far as she was concerned her grandmother had sent Johnny Cake off and that was the end of it.

Johnny Cake came over the next day to pick Quinty up. It so happened that Tilla and her grandmother had gone to visit a family member and would not be back until the following day, so Quinty had the place all to herself. She well and knew that when she told Johnny to call back at the house! When Johnny Cake knocked at the door, she invited him in.

"Oh, we noh haffi go out now," she said.

"Mama an Killa gaan look fi me cousin an nah come back til a marnin."

"Come in…" Quinty stepped aside just enough for him to squeeze past her.

"Oh bwoy!" Johnny thought to himself as he reluctantly stepped inside.

Quinty showed him into her section of the house. She had a sumptuous bedroom, a beautifully decorated living room, a well-stocked kitchen and an en-suite shower room. Johnny Cake was nervous. He would have preferred to meet Quinty in a public place so that he could feel more in control of things. Quinty assured Johhny Cake that if Tilla and Miss Sour Sop came home unexpectedly he would not be seen. She reminded him Miss Sour Sop told him not to come back! Johnny Cake felt uncomfortable. Quinty smelled divine and she looked fabulous in her feminine and floaty summer dress. He dragged his thoughts back to the present, and why he was there. Johnny Cake knew it was going to be hard to remain professional, but he really wanted to sign Tilla. He decided being alone with Quinty was a risk he would have to take. If he could show Quinty that her daughter had a future in the music industry, maybe she would be able to persuade Miss Sour Sop to change her mind. Well, he thought, she was the girl's mother after all...

Quinty showed Johnny Cake into her living room and told him to make himself comfortable on her plush sofa. She poured him a soft drink, as he said he was driving and needed to keep a clear head. She smiled to herself, because she knew why he was so eager to keep a clear head.

She sat on the sofa next to him, very close so that he could smell her perfume, their thighs touching. Johnny was trapped. He could not move away from her without making it look obvious. He had to play it cool. "So, Mr Johnny Cake, how you plan fi launch mi daughter career?"

Johnny cleared his throat and started to explain. Quinty relaxed beside him, looking into his eyes attentively. Looking at her made him giddy. She urged him to take off his jacket, as he seemed to be getting very hot. She got up to hang it up and her hand brushed his, sending a shiver down his spine. She swished her hips slightly while she walked over to the other side of the room to hang the jacket up. As she walked back towards Johnny Cake, she looked deep into his eyes, her top half jiggled slightly (I can't say breasts, that's rude!), and he noticed. He silently crossed himself and prayed.
"Lawd, deliver me!" He said to himself.
"Me inna heap a trouble now."
Johnny Cake willed himself to stay in control and concentrate on the task in hand.
"Mr Johnny Cake, continue please...what you sayin' now bout Killa?"
"Er, yes, well..." He stammered.
Quinty sat down again very close to Johnny Cake. As she sat down, she leaned back in the settee, and urged him to do the same.
"Relax Mr Cake, or me can call you Johnny?"
"Ow you so stiff?" She frowned.
"Me nah bite you."
Then she laughed quietly.
"Alrite, come now, and explain how tings ah go run..."
She turned to face Johnny Cake and her [top half] jiggled again. Johnny Cake had nowhere to turn! He felt hot. Quinty smiled innocently. He noticed she had a lovely smile. His eyes could not help but wander downwards. Something stirred in him which made him suddenly go weak and his mouth feel dry. Quinty parted her smooth, long legs ever so slightly. It was a tiny movement, but Johnny Cake noticed it just the same.

"Oh, it so hot in here. You noh tink so?" Quinty said as she leaned forward slightly.

(If you have a weak disposition please stop reading now and move on to the next story. Actually don't, because the next story is no better! You may as well continue).

Johnny Cake froze. He realised then that he was foolish to think he could manage being so close to Quinty without it having an effect on him. He knew that she knew what she was doing, but she was so damned hard to resist! He could feel Quinty's voice, soft in his ear, her lips almost brushing his neck.

"Mr Cake, you alrite?"

"You want me loosen you tie?"

"You look like you struggling to breathe..."

She did not wait for a response before leaning over to unbutton the neck of his shirt. In a quick movement, she slipped her hand inside and touched his chest lightly.

"Oh dear," she said

"You burning up Mr Cake!"

"Sorry, di air conditioning been playin' up all marnin."

"I tink you need some assistance...let me help you get some air...."

Her eyes travelled from his chest downwards and she smiled.

"I see now where the air transfer to."

Later that evening Quinty was on the phone to a friend.
"Well, mek ah tell you, Johnny Cake figget bout money an' contrak when me lean ova him to boxfront!"

Both women collapsed in fits of laughter. It took a few minutes to get back her composure.

"Me ah go call 'im tomorrow." She said.

"Him lef 'im briefcase, an 'im tie!"

Big laugh buss out again.

"Woooyyy, Quinty. You too bad!" Her friend exclaimed.
"But wait," the friend said.
"You ah go mek Tilla sign contrak?"
"Contrak whah?!!" Quinty retorted, and she kissed her teeth.

Quinty smiled to herself, put on her favourite Johnny Osbourne song "In Your Eyes" and turned the volume up.

CORNMEAL TUN OVA!!

Turna Cornmeal had been single for about six months; since she was held responsible for spreading the rumour that Chris Cassava was a virgin with a small buddy. Even her oldest friend, the amiable Fiona Festival, was refusing to talk to her.

Turna thought about their last conversation.
"But Turna, you outa order eeehh!" Fiona scolded.
"Ow you know anyway?" She added.
"Ah noh so it go!" Turna responded.
"Well 'ow it go den?" Fiona fired back.
Turna began to explain.
"Look, me jus' mention me notice seh me neva see him wid anybaddy, and me ah wonder hef true seh him inna de church if him a keep himself pure fi him future wife. Das all me seh!"
"Lie you lie!" Fiona accused.
"Talk di trute. How him buddy get inna de argument?" Turna shrugged her shoulders.
"Well, me did ongle crack a likkle joke 'bout me woulda dead wid laugh if him wife did bad lucky enough fi get small offerings from inna di 'collection box' pon de marriage night."
"An das all me seh!" Turna tried to look sincere.
"Anyway, you know Mrs Fung weh own de carner shop?" Turna continued.
"She mussi hear me ah talk, an' nex ting me know story spread like butter pon slice mongoose bread dat me ah call de man likkle buddy virgin."
"Bwoy, it come in like Chinese whisper fi true!" Turna shrugged her shoulders.
Fiona Fistival was not amused.
"Turna, you know seh Cock mout kill Cock?"

"You mus' learn fi kibba you mout, it too long!"

Turna pouted, feeling chastised. She shouldn't have joked about Chris Cassava in that way, she just couldn't help herself. She knew Fiona Festival had always liked Chris, and she knew he liked Fiona too, but they were both skirting around each other, none of them wanting to make the first move. Turna could have intervened to bring the two of them together before now, but she didn't because she was jealous, although she could not admit it to herself. Deep down she didn't want Fiona to find happiness because she herself had not, and you know the saying, 'two's company three's a crowd'. So Turna was not in any hurry to pair her friend up with the man who would take her attention away. Turna was behaving very selfishly. She wasn't that bothered about making fun of Chris, even though it upset Fiona.

"Alright Fiona, cho!" Turna said.
"Me know you like him, but me neva mean notn."
"How you know?" Fiona asked, surprised.
"Me know fram long time." Turna owned up.
Fiona was vexed.
"So wait…if you know dat, why you go faas an trouble de man? Caah you see me look pon 'im you haffi trouble weh noh trouble you!"
"Bwoy Turna, you bad mind!"
Turna tried to placate Fiona.
"Alright noh Fiona, noh badda gwaan so. Ah no notn. Man ah dahg!"
"Beg you parden!" Fiona raised her voice.
"Is who you ah call dahg?" This was the last straw.
"Not dat man Turna!"
"Noh da one deh!"

Fiona was hurt. She had put up with Turna's gossiping ways for years, since they were children. Now she believed Turna had sunk to a new low by making fun of the man Fiona was secretly in love with and whom she fantasised about marrying whenever she passed a wedding shop or when she heard someone was getting married. Up until that day, Fiona always felt sorry for Turna, because she sensed a sadness in her that she masked with her behaviour. But now she couldn't help but remember the old saying, "Sorry fi mahga dawg, mahga dawg tun round bite you." Fiona resolved that she would not speak to Turna until she saw the error of her ways and apologised. She was going to teach her a lesson. Silent river run deep (a quiet person shouldn't be taken for a fool).

"You know wha?" Fiona pointed her finger at Turna. "Argument done! No badda even call me."
"Memba me seh...Same ting weh tick sheep, tick goat!"
And with that Fiona turned and walked away without another word.

The males in the district were keeping their distance from Turna Cornmeal since the Cassava scandal, apart from Maas Run Down (cho, go siddung, you pass you prime!). Turna was lonely and frustrated. She decided that if Fiona was determined to pursue Chris Cassava, then she needed to find herself a boyfriend too. The trouble was the local males didn't appeal to her because the community was small and everybody knew everybody. Or rather, everyone in the community knew how she labba labba and two faced, and Cassava-gate was still fresh in people's minds. Turna had really messed up this time. Chris Cassava was a popular person in the village and everybody loved Fiona Festival. The residents were very unhappy with Turna Cornmeal or Turn-Coat as they now labelled her. She knew that she would have to look outside of her neighbourhood to find companionship, at least until things had died down. She cheered herself up by imagining her next beau to be someone handsome, virile, confident, generous to a fault, loaded and exciting!

Turna began frequenting out of town venues and places of interest, trying to meet new people. After a couple of months, she began to get tired of the search, as it wasn't throwing up what she expected. She did meet a couple of men but one lived with his mother and still slept in a single bed from his childhood, and his mother insisted Turna remained on the front veranda when she visited. The other guy was a gorgeous body builder who spent most of the time looking at his reflection in every shiny surface he came across and would not invite Turna to his place, even though he said he lived alone. He claimed he worked, but never seemed to have any money and miraculously forgot or lost his wallet the few times they went out. Very soon, she was back to square one. She was fed up. No man, no relationship. Then she hit upon an idea…

A friend had told her how she used a discreet escort agency whenever she wanted a short-term fix, or required some eye-candy on her arm for important social functions, when she was between boyfriends. The friend said the service she received was always excellent. Turna was intrigued. She decided to give it a try. She was excited by the prospect of 100% satisfaction guaranteed! She called the agency and registered under a different name. She could pretend, at least for one night, that she had a boyfriend. She told the agency her exact requirements and they assured her they had just the man she needed.

On the appointed night she arrived at the arranged location, which was a nice hotel with comfortable, elegantly styled rooms. Turna was beside herself with excitement. She dimmed the lights and made herself comfortable, having followed the instructions she had been given by the agency, and waited for her pick 'n' mix man to arrive. While she waited, she adjusted her wig and checked her make-up. She was trying to disguise herself as an added precaution. She didn't wait for long. He entered the room wearing a mask; the kind that you wear to a masquerade ball. He had on a black Armani suit, criss white shirt unbuttoned to his chest, which was smooth like dark chocolate and he smelled divine!! Turna melted in anticipation. He told her his name was Carlton. She knew it wasn't his real name but she didn't care. They engaged in small talk, and then he leaned over turned the lights down lower…

That night Turna saw the whole galaxy of stars. She visited Jupiter and Mars. She walked on the Moon and went to Heaven and back! By the end of the night she was speaking in tongues! Eventually it was time to end the session and Carlton got up to prepare to leave. He had removed his mask and when he turned the light up Turna was able to see his face. They looked at each other and froze….

"Lawd!!" Exclaimed Turna.
She could now see clearly who "Carlton" was, and she was mortified. It was local pretty boy Cliff Cowcod. She couldn't stand him because she thought he was buff but she got the impression he thought he was too

good for her. She remembered how she approached him one time and tried to make small talk, but he acted so aloof and made her feel she was trying way too hard. She declared to her friends at the time "Scornful dawg nyam dutty pudding", which means he's going on too fussy, which will be his downfall. Now she had actually paid for his services, and thoroughly enjoyed herself, and she felt shame!

Cliff himself was also in shock. This was the labba mouth woman the residents had warned him about when he moved to the neighbourhood. Now she was aware of what he did for a living on the down low! How was he going salvage his reputation and keep his part time job a secret with Big Mouth in a position to expose him?! Before he could answer his own question, he became aware that she was saying something to him.
"Listen Mr Cowcod, dis a dreadful mistake."
"Me ah aks you fi no badda tell no baddy 'bout tonight." She continued.
"After all, me sure nobaddy noh know 'bout you likkle side line." She paused a little to labour the point.
 "An' you noh waan nobaddy fi know eider, me sure of dat."

"Well Miss Turna, me glad seh you agree fi jus' let matters rest right here, an' noh go noh furder." He replied.
"So, I bid you good night."
And with that he hastily left, relieved that he had enough evidence on her to prevent her from telling others about him without incriminating herself.
Actually, he thought it was a good thing that she had enjoyed his 'company' tonight. He could use it as leverage to curb her bad mind, gossiping ways.

Turna, meanwhile, was thinking about what took place as she got dressed. She was so embarrassed; she couldn't bear it if the story got out.
"Lard, me caant believe it." She said to herself.
"How me ah go live dis down?"
"Me mek dat stoosh, facety bwoy tun me front an' back, up an dung. Wooyy, what a ting!"
She held her head in her hands. Eventually, she had to admit to herself that, despite the circumstances, he was damn good at his job! Oh, but the shame! Cliff Cowcod of all people now knew her all her intimate secrets. She determined she had to try to mend her bad ways, as surely this was Karma. As she tidied up the hotel room, she pondered how she was going to keep her composure when she saw him again.
Now, that's another story….

PRICKLY PEAR GETS PRICKED

Mrs Pear is a forty-something staunch, church-going, god-fearing (so she seh!) woman. She acquired the nickname Prickly Pear due to her stuck-up, haughty behaviour. Her husband left her about six years ago and ran off with her church sister, Miss Winifred. For years before that the two women had been inseparable. They were in and out of each other's homes daily, and were always on the phone to each other (a labrish an' a chat people business). People used to call them Batty an' Cheek, because you wouldn't see one without the other. Anyway, it so happens that, unbeknown to Mrs Pear, Miss Winifred had designs on her husband (Hmm! Weh me tell you 'bout church people?!). Miss Winifred overlooked the fact that she should not covet the possessions of another (although a husband/wife is not a possession – certain people would argue otherwise). She also skipped over the Commandment that she should not commit adultery. Well, one day Mrs Pear came home from church to find her husband, Brother Pear, had disappeared. When she looked in his wardrobe all Brother Pear's clothes had gone. She looked in his drawers and they were mostly empty, with only old unwanted clothes left behind.

She got on the phone to tell her friend Sister Winifred, but the line was disconnected. When she went around to Sister Winifred's house it was locked up and it was clear there was no-one home. Mrs Pear remembered her husband saying he was too ill to go with her to church that morning. She also recalled Sister Winifred telling her she had to travel out of town unexpectedly so she couldn't come to church. However, Prickly

Pear did not put two and two together. Why should she? She was far too proud and certain of herself to even imagine that her simpleton husband who of course adored her so much and dutifully carried out every task required of him, would run off with someone else, especially one of her church sisters.

So, what did Mrs Pear do? She went down to the local police station and reported him missing, of course. The officers asked a few cursory questions, and quickly came to the conclusion that he had run off with Sister Winifred, which they wasted no time in telling Mrs Pear very bluntly (as Jamaicans do). It was easy, actually, to come to that conclusion because Chris Cassava, who happened to work at the station, saw Brother Pear and Sister Winifred getting into her car and driving off at high speed earlier that morning, as if they were in a hurry to get somewhere. He couldn't help but share the news when he got to work. It was an exclusive! The gossip circled the parish twice before the church service done! What a way bad news travel faas!

Prickley Pear's visit to the police station that afternoon didn't go very well. In true Jamaican style Officer Dibble offered a sympathetic ear.
"Mrs Pear. Sister Winifred gaan, you osban' gaan. Weh you tink dat mean?"
"Dat is what I want you to find out, Officer!" Prickly Pear replied.
"Me noh so worried 'bout Sister Winifred, caah she gaan ah she family, but me 'osban disappear which 'im neva do before."
"Unnu need fi go look fi 'im!" She was becoming distraught.
"Mrs Pear." Officer Dibble was in a patient mood.

"How long 'im missing for?"
"Me noh know…'bout 3 hour now since me discover 'im gaan."
Officer Dibble raised his eyes to the ceiling, sighed and turned towards Prickly Pear. His patience had run out.
"Mrs Pear. Me ah go pon me lunch break in two minutes. So, me ah tell you weh me know now, fi save time an' energy weh me don' 'ave dis afternoon, okay."
"You have a lead…?" Prickly Pear was hopeful.
"Yes, me 'ave a lead. A dawg lead." Officer Dibble replied.
Prickly Pear was confused. Officer Dibble continued speaking.
"You so called fait'ful osban run gaan wid Sister Winifred while you deh ah church. So me a gi' you a dawg lead; fi tie 'im up when 'im come back so 'im caan get weh again."

Prickly Pear was indignant at the accusations levelled at her husband by the police, whom she had approached for help in her hour of need. She should have known they would not take her plight seriously. She marched out of the station and went back home, where she wrote a strong letter of complaint about the shoddy way her case had been dealt with.

Prickly Pear didn't get much sympathy from the local community after her husband's disappearance. That's because she used to go on so boasty about her "osban". She was forever saying "my osban" this and "my osban" that. It wasn't funny when people in the district got to hear about poor Mrs Pear's misfortune losing her "osban" to Miss Winifred. The elders repeated the well-known phrase "Same ting weh tick sheep, tick goat!" (the same thing that happens to someone else can happen to you).

Quinty Dumpling drew her own conclusion, "If she neva gwaan so stoosh neegle eye wouldn' steal she osban."

Prickly Pear felt so shame her "osban" had run off with someone else; but then she did used to look down and 'pass remark' on other women because they had no husband or ring on their finger. So, she made up a story she would repeat to anyone who would listen. It was that her husband's mother had taken ill and he had to leave in a hurry to go and care for her. That was six years ago and the man hasn't been seen since! Neither has her 'good fren' Winifred. (Noh worry you-self, reader. Me noh done yet wid de elusive Mr Pear and double-crossing, clean-up woman Miss Winifred. Res dat story here fi now.)

Cliff Cowcod has just moved into the neighbourhood. He is very good looking, dark and handsome. All the women are excited as he seems very eligible. He tells them he is single, and he is. What he doesn't tell them is that he does private work as a male escort for women who can afford him. His other pastime is seducing, I mean romancing, women who are in the church. It's a strange fetish. I think it stems from when he was a boy going to church and he would see the goings on during the service; the women flinging themselves about, shaking themselves up and down, muttering in tongues, calling out as if in ecstasy. It fascinated him. As he grew older the memory never left him. He thought to himself, "If I could have ONE woman respond to me like that, I would be the happiest man in town!" And that's how it all began. Since he has been doing his (ahem!) part time side-line, he has been surprised at the number of church-going females who have requested his services. He knows they go to church because they tend to recite bible verses loudly and pray a lot for their pastor not to find out and for the Almighty to forgive them! He loves church women because in his opinion they are the most 'expressive' and vocal, shall we say. I digress! Back to the story.

Cliff Cowcod's part time job really pays dividends; a nice shirt, a pair of shoes he has had his eye on, the latest aftershave. These are just a few of the gifts he has received. That's not including his tips and his booking fee. The wealthier women are the most generous, he finds. One bought him a car. Another one financed a nice holiday with spending money thrown in. Cliff has to let them down gently when they start hinting about exclusive dating. When things get too hot to handle, he has to leave town quick! He has just moved on again and has a new hunting ground. His eyes are firmly set on the prize in this new neighbourhood; and the prize is…Mrs Prickly Pear!

Prickly Pear felt lonely, but she would never admit it to anyone. Going to church was all very well, but church could not fill the void in her life that a man could. She had realised that about two years after her 'osban' went off to care for his mother (she still ah repeat dat foolishness?!). Pastor Lickie Lickie always preaches to the congregation that the Saviour can satisfy every need.
"Me no tink so!" Is always Quinty Dumpling's response. When Prickly Pear's 'osban' was around she truly believed Pastor Lickie Lickie, but since she has been on her own, she isn't so sure. Her 'un-Christian' conscience told her in a loud voice "YOU NEED A MAN!" Her Christian conscience reminded her, "Thou shalt not commit adultery."

"Hmm," she thought.
"De man gaan lef me, an me ah siddung ah wait fi so long. Cho!"
But she just couldn't bring her stoosh self to do anything about it. In fact, she didn't know *what* to do. Okay, okay, she did know what to do, but she pretended to herself that she didn't because she was afraid of God intercepting her sinful thoughts...

The following day, Prickly Pear was standing at her kitchen window, which happened to face the street, when she saw a removal van pull up. The van came to a halt at the empty house next door, and out jumped the handsomest man she had ever seen. He was dark with smouldering looks and a physique to match. He was gorgeous! Prickly Pear found herself staring. She turned away quickly and chastised herself for being a mortal sinner. This must be the new neighbour, she thought. Something inside her stirred. She had a funny feeling in the pit of her stomach which she did not recognise. She felt all warm, so she went and turned up the air conditioning! She went back to the window to sneak another look; she couldn't help herself.

The new neighbour was helping the removal men to unload and move his belongings into his new home. At one stage he looked up as if he could sense someone watching him, but Prickly Pear thought she was well hidden behind her curtain. All the same, she didn't dare move. She could feel him looking at her. She came over all goosepimples. He went back to moving in and soon the removal van was empty and he had gone inside the house. There had been talk in the church about someone renting the house next door, which had recently been vacated by a young couple who had returned to the USA. Prickly Pear was not normally shy, but she could not bring herself to go and knock to introduce herself as his new neighbour. She was usually the first to go and introduce herself (as the self-appointed moral guardian of the neighbourhood) to new-comers, presenting them with a small container of ackee and saltfish, her speciality dish, as a gift. Now, though, she felt like a silly schoolgirl.

Cliff Cowcod could not see Prickly Pear when he had looked up at her window, but he could sense she was standing there behind her curtains watching him. He smiled to himself. The game had already begun. He was looking forward to this challenge; she was so uptight and this would take a little more effort. However, the rewards, he was sure, would be worth it. He had come to view the property a couple of weeks ago, and had asked about his new neighbour. He was given the low-down on how she was alone since her husband left her...sorry, since he went to go look after his mother. Cliff was excited at the prospect of getting to know the haughty Mrs Prickly Pear.

One day Prickly Pear needed to get some groceries. She came out of her house to make her way to the bus stop to go into town. Cliff Cowcod saw her come out and hesitate on the veranda. He decided to make his move. He came out to his front porch pretending to look over the property checking for minor repairs that needed doing. He feigned surprise to see her.
"Oh, marnin neighbour!" He said.
"Good mawning." She replied crisply.
Cliff wasn't put off.
"Pleased to make your acquaintance, I am Cliff, how do you do?" He said.

"Very well, thank you. I am Mrs Pear."
Cliff went over to her and they shook hands. Prickly Pear's heart skipped a beat.
"Have you lived in the area very long?" Cliff asked, already knowing the answer.

Prickly Pear explained that she had lived there most of her life. They exchanged some more pleasantries before she set off down the road towards the bus stop. Cliff watched her as she went. He could tell he had the desired effect on her. He smiled to himself. She was conscious that he was watching her as she walked. Her head felt light and her legs felt like jelly.

Over the next few weeks Cliff continued to wear down Prickly Pear's defences and they got on really well. She invited him to church as her guest, and he obliged a few times. She enjoyed the envious stares she received from the female members of the congregation, and even a couple of the men...but we won't go there!

After getting to know Prickly Pear, Cliff began to hatch a plan. He knew Prickly Pear loved her garden. She didn't know much about plants but she loved flowers, and she paid a gardener to maintain her garden. Cliff told her how he loved flowers also and he loved to go hunting for new species. He could tell that this sparked her interest that they had something in common. Then, he went and bought a small yellow shrub that was not commonly grown in their area and planted it carefully in a secluded spot in the bush at the end of the road. He waited until it was dark, then went to Prickly Pear feigning excitement, and told her he had discovered a rare plant in the bush that glowed in the dark which he wanted to show her (oldest trick in

the book, this one!). Prickly Pear was intrigued. She thought to herself how good it would be to show off that rare plant in her own garden, and be the envy of her neighbours. Cliff asked her to come quickly, to see the plant before someone else found it or insects chewed it. At first, she protested, saying it was too dark. He assured her they would be perfectly safe, and urged her to come quickly. She followed him gingerly while they made their way through the shrubbery. The conversation went like this:
"There it is..." Cliff pointed.
"Where?"
"Over here....You haffi ben ova likkle more fi see it"
(Rustling noises)
"Me ciant see notn..."
"Shhh...Look properly, Mrs Pear. Mek me show you...Right down 'ere."
"Ben down lower Mrs Pear, you noh have you glasses?!"
"I don't need no glasses!"
"Well, you should be able to see it den."
"Me see it, me see it!" Mrs Pear squeeled with joy
"Smell it noh... It smell lovely..." Cliff encouraged her.
"Oh yes, it do.....but Mr Cowcod, it no 'ave much glow.."
"Das funny, Mrs Pear. You right. It don' 'ave much glow now I tink bout it."
(More rustling noises)
"Oh, Mr Cowcod...I feel someting strange crawling up mi leg!"
"Stay calm Mrs Pear. Mek me feel an see what it is. Stay still...it could be a poisonous insek."
"Mr Cowcod, it feel like it goin' inna mi drawers!"
"Hold on Mrs Pear, me tink a likkle harmless snake..."
"SNAKE! HELP! Tek it out Mr Cowcod!"

"Please Mrs Pear keep calm! You haffi stay still. I jus' goin' try use me piece a wood and tek it out."
"Woy!!"
"Easy, Mrs Pear. Easy does it. Me jus' a tease it out gently, in-case it bite. Keep quiet and deadly still. This might take a minute or two...."
"That's wonderful Mrs Pear."
(Heavy breathing)
"I tink I have 'im now."
(More heavy breathing)
"Lovely. You doin really well Mrs Pear. Almost there. Look like 'im noh waan come out."
(More rustling noises, and muffled moaning)

Maas Run Down was making his way to work at the local police station (Blimey, look like everyone works at the bleedin' station!). He tells potential girlfriends/conquests that he works for an important organisation, which in itself is no lie. That always makes them think he must be somebody high up and they start seeing dollar signs. Maas Run Down is actually a cleaner at the police station, but he calls himself a Sanitary Manager. You know people love to make like they are in big job because they don't want to feel small. Anyway, Maas Run Down was walking to work and took a little-used short cut through the same bush where Prickly Pear and Cliff Cowcod were. While walking he heard strange groaning and rustling noises which at first frightened the life out of him. A short time later on his arrival at work he told the following story.

"....Den she shout "Oh my Saviour, oh my Saviour!" Me noh know wha' kine ah spirit tek her, but it shake de mango off de tree an mek dem bonks down pon de ground like rain a fall. Next ting me hear, she baahl out "whooooy, whooooy!" Me sure seh ah man she did deh wid! But me could'n see too well."

At that point his co-workers at the station began to cuss him loudly, complaining that 'im chat to raaas claaat much. How could he even think that Mrs Prickly Pear would entertain a strange man in the bushes like that. Mrs Prickly Pear?! No, they couldn't even imagine it. They concluded Mass Run Down had clearly lost his mind momentarily and needed a reality check. So, the Sargent threatened to sack him, if him noh shut 'im diamn, fool-fool, yabba yabba mout' an go clean out de toilet.

The next day Prickly Pear was not to be seen. Apparently, she called one of her church sisters and told her she had had a restless night and was too tired to attend evening prayers.

Oh, Mrs Prickly Pear! Looks like she's not so prickly after all. What you have to do is carefully peel away the outside skin, in order to reach the juicy flesh inside.

Acknowledgements

Big shout out to my family, The Richards, who originate from Guava Ground, Clarendon, Jamaica WI. Also, the Calliard clan, who hail from Trelawny, Jamaica WI. To my parents, without whom I would not be here today! To my children, who continue to endure my wacky sense of humour. To my godchildren (Aaron, Emile, Aliyah - and their siblings) who love me regardless, and my grandchildren (Owen and Gabriel) whose smiles and laughter mean so much to me. To my friends, including the Kidbrooke Massive, Lunch Ladies, Holiday Girls, the NPS Crew, and especially the 'Committee Members' – now you know what I've been up to and why I've been AWOL in recent months! Forgive me for keeping the book a secret. To Cousin Shirley, who helped with my research without knowing it! To Jacqs and Auj, and cousin Pat (whose humour is drier than the Sahara Desert!) for regaling me with humorous stories about our family. To Big Cousin Sil, who was the best at telling funny stories. I so loved to listen to him. Rest in eternal peace. To Natasha, for her help and advice. To Sue Brown, for those sessions that pushed me forward. To Donna (Jackson), thank you for sharing and putting things into perspective. To all the individuals who have made me laugh and lifted my spirits over the years. And those who made me cry; it made me rise up stronger and more determined. Finally, thank you to G Sloley for his encouragement and support, which helped me to plough on and get the book finished...at last.

It has been a labour of love. Sometimes all-consuming, at times frustrating, at other times a hopeless task I feared I would never complete. I've been hindered by numerous distractions, including fear (of failure, or even success), self-doubt, and downright laziness!

It has taken 20 odd years to get to this stage; since the day I decided I was going to start writing and one day have my work published. Granted, I didn't expect it to take two decades but, as the saying goes, nothing happens before the time. I personally would not advise leaving it so long to fulfil your dreams! So, if you have a burning desire to achieve a particular goal, don't delay. The time is now.

References

Higman, B. W. and Hudson, B. J. (2009). Jamaican Place Names. Mona, Jamaica: University of the West Indies Press. P. 31.

Wikipedia:
https://en.wikipedia.org/wiki/Parishes_of_Jamaica

Henry, L. M. and Harris, K. S. (2006) LMH Official Dictionary of Jamaican Words & Proverbs, 3rd Ed. Kingston, Jamaica: LMH Publishing Ltd.

Jamaica Information Service at:
https://jis.gov.jm/information/parish-profiles/

Printed in Poland
by Amazon Fulfillment
Poland Sp. z o.o., Wrocław